the semicolon

written by Britt Sayler

illustrated by Dorota Rewerenda

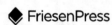 FriesenPress

One Printers Way
Altona, MB R0G 0B0
Canada

www.friesenpress.com

Copyright © 2022 by Britt Sayler
First Edition — 2022

Illustrated by Dorota Rewerenda

ISBN
978-1-03-912067-9 (Hardcover)
978-1-03-912066-2 (Paperback)
978-1-03-912068-6 (eBook)

I. JUVENILE FICTION, FAMILY, PARENTS

Distributed to the trade by
The Ingram Book Company

The dream came after Dad left.

Every night, a giant pit sucked and slurped up everything.

And every night, it slurped me up, too.

I missed Dad
more than anything.

One day, *rat-a-tat-tat!* It was Dad's old teaching buddy, Mr. Smeechie. He had something of Dad's for me.

I'd always wished Dad had been something cooler than a grammar teacher.

"Oh, ho!" said Mr. Smeechie at my expression. "Grammar is important! Without it, words would fly everywhere. Nothing would make sense!"

I couldn't put my own words together to tell Mr. Smeechie that nothing made sense anyway.

"See these quotation marks?"
Mr. Smeechie drew on a piece of paper.

"They scoop out the air like ice cream to make room for what you want to say."

"Periods are black holes that suck up sound until you are a safe distance away!"

"Commas are *rafts* that ferry  one idea to another."

I pointed to a funny mark Dad had circled in red ink.
It had both the dot of a period and the wave of a comma.

"That," said Mr. Smeechie, "was your dad's *favourite symbol of all*." Then he looked at his watch and whoops, Mr. Smeechie had to go.

That night, I dreamed once more of the pit. It looked just like the period Mr. Smeechie had described. A period meant something was over.

Finished.

Done.

Introduction to GRAMMAR

And like the black hole of a period,
it slurped up everything it could reach,
including me.

The next night, I had a solution to my pit problem.

Never sleeping again didn't work as well as I'd hoped.

This time at the pit, I was not alone. The symbols from Dad's grammar book were there with me.

I scrambled for safety on top of a question mark.

But the pit swallowed it like a strand of spaghetti.

I tried tying quotation marks together to make a rope.

But the pit devoured those, knots and all.

One symbol was not getting slurped away like the rest.
Mr. Smeechie had called commas the rafts that ferried
one idea to another. Could it carry me, too?

I put one foot on.

It wobbled but didn't sink.

I stepped on completely.

I had a funny feeling that

maybe

it had been there *all along.*

Suddenly, the comma took off across the oozy, black surface.

It floated even when the pit's slurping became a *roar* and inky bubbles *splashed my toes.*

Further and further it carried me, until I couldn't see where I'd started.

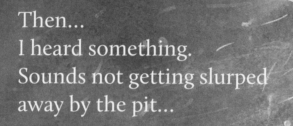

Then...
I heard something.
Sounds not getting slurped
away by the pit...

Laughter.

Voices.

Dad's voice.

And drifting closer, I had a bigger surprise...

V

I saw the soccer ball Dad and I used to play
with. I heard the cheer he made each time
I scored a goal. I saw the new girl on the
bus who I wanted to sit beside, the one
Dad always told me I should talk to.

Beyond the pit were memories of Dad and me,
and possibilities yet to come.

The dream left
after the grammar
book came.

The next day, I went to visit Mr. Smeechie. "What does that funny symbol mean?" I asked. My own words made sense again.

Mr. Smeechie smiled and wrote two sentences on the board. He placed the funny symbol between them. "This is called a *semicolon*," he said. "Sometimes things like sentences seem as if they are over, but really, there is more that comes afterwards. When that happens, we use a semicolon instead of a period."

He handed me a pencil so
I could try.

I looked at the semicolon. I saw
the black pit that seemed at
the time like it would suck and
slurp up everything. But I also
saw the comma, the raft that
meant there was a way across...
and something to cross to.

Now I understood why
that funny symbol was
Dad's favourite.

I thanked Mr. Smeechie and took my soccer
ball to the park where Dad and I used to play;

author's note

Thank you for reading *The Semicolon!* This story means a lot to me. I hope it will mean something to you, too.

As with most books, people find different meanings in *The Semicolon.* For some readers, it's a story about grief after loss. For others, it's an un-boring introduction to grammar and punctuation.

For me, this story has always been about depression and mental health. Like the protagonist in *The Semicolon,* it is not only adults who are susceptible to depression. Experts believe as many as 1 in 30 children under the age of 12 have serious depression. Countless children will grow up to experience depression themselves or in loved ones.

Depression is different from the normal sadness or sense of disconnect that all of us feel from time to time. In *The Semicolon,* the protagonist is grieving the loss of their father, but their grief has also turned into depression. They no longer smile. They are not interested in playing their favourite sport, soccer. Inside, they feel scared, sick, angry and lonely. And at night, their pain takes the form of a dark, slurping pit that seems as though it will swallow them whole.

For both children and adults, it can be hard to explain what we are going through when we are depressed, even to ourselves. At the beginning of the story, the protagonist is unable to speak to their friend, Mr. Smeechie. The protagonist has so many overwhelming and confusing feelings that they do not know how to put them into words.

The protagonist ultimately finds hope from the symbols in their father's old grammar book, especially the semicolon. For many people who have experienced depression, the semicolon is special because it means *there is more to come.* For the protagonist, the pit seemed so huge and powerful that, at first, they could not imagine anything past it. Yet their journey on the comma reveals that there is still life, with all its good things, on the other side of their pain. This simple reminder that our story is not over (no matter how much it may feel otherwise!) has made the semicolon an inspiration to millions of people around the world.

I hope this book will add to important conversations about mental health and well-being. For my younger readers, I hope this book will be like a cozy sweater to grow into, which you can always pull out for a rainy day.

Much love,
britt sayler

about the author

Britt Sayler is a writer originally from Calgary, Canada, who is thrilled to make her picture book debut with *The Semicolon*. She holds a Graduate Certificate in Creative Writing from Humber College and has worked as a magazine editor and freelance writer across the country. Britt has twice been longlisted in the national CANSCAIP Writing for Children competition (2018 and 2020), including for an earlier version of this story. She was compelled to write about the difficult topic of childhood depression after navigating her own challenges with mental health and learning that 1 in 30 children within the average age range of picture book readers is currently depressed. Britt writes for both children and adults, and lives with a rescue dog who makes an appearance in *The Semicolon!*

To learn more, visit www.brittsaylerbooks.com.

Printed in the USA
CPSIA information can be obtained
at www.ICGtesting.com
LVHW071739101023
760723LV00009B/25